THE STORY OF GULLIVER

JONATHAN COE

Illustrated by
Sara Oddi

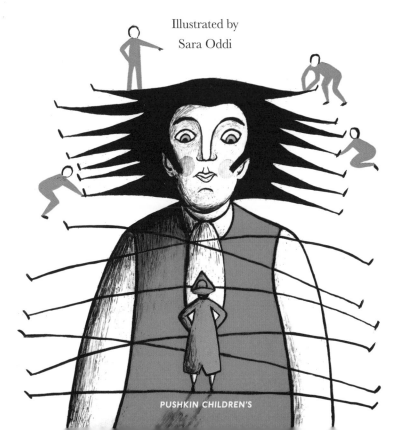

PUSHKIN CHILDREN'S

Pushkin Press
71–75 Shelton Street
London WC2H 9JQ

The Story of Gulliver was first published as
La storia di Gulliver in Italy, 2011

First published by Pushkin Press in 2013
This paperback edition first published in 2018

9 8 7 6 5 4 3 2 1

ISBN 13: 978-1-78269-207-2

Set in Garamond Premier Pro by Tetragon, London

Printed and bound in Italy by Printer Trento

www.pushkinpress.com

MIX
Paper from
responsible sources
FSC® C015829

THE STORY OF GULLIVER

One

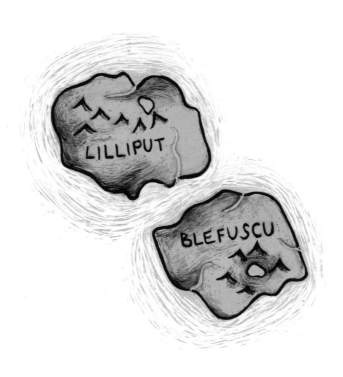

Almost 300 years ago, there lived a man with a strange name. His name was Lemuel Gulliver.

Gulliver worked as a doctor on board the great ships that left England and sailed around the world in order to buy and sell goods in other countries. It was dangerous work. The seas were sometimes rough and stormy, and the ships often sailed to places which were unknown to the sailors and were not marked on any map.

At home in England, Gulliver had a wife and children. But he needed to travel on these long voyages in order to make money and, besides, he had a great love of travelling, and a great curiosity to see new places.

This is the story of Gulliver's travels: travels which would lead him to discover four amazing new countries, and would change the way he felt about his fellow human beings for ever.

Gulliver's first voyage was in the year 1699. His ship set sail from Bristol and made for the West Indies. It was a very long journey. Then, after six months' sailing, the ship met with a terrible accident. It ran aground against an enormous rock in the middle of the ocean, and it was completely destroyed.

Many of the sailors died, but Gulliver managed to swim to the shore of a strange island. As soon as he dragged himself onto the beach he fell asleep, exhausted.

When he woke up, many hours later, he found that he was lying on his back and couldn't move. He was tied down by hundreds of strong threads, and even his hair had been tied to the ground. The sun was so bright in his eyes that he could hardly see. Then Gulliver felt something crawling along his chest. He looked down, expecting to see an insect or a mouse, but was astonished to see something completely different. It was a tiny man, dressed in fine and elegant clothes, but standing no taller than a pencil! The man was being followed along Gulliver's chest by almost forty companions. When Gulliver saw them, he roared with fright so loudly that many of the little men fell off his body onto the hard, sandy beach and hurt themselves.

By pulling at the threads, Gulliver managed to free one of his arms and turn his head a little bit. Immediately, the men drew out their weapons and fired tiny arrows at his face. They stung like pins and needles, and he cried out in pain. Now he could easily have killed one of the tiny men, but he had no wish to do that. So instead he made a sign to say that he meant them no harm. They understood, and they put a ladder and a wooden platform next to his ear so that they could climb up and talk to him.

A spokesman then made a long speech in his own peculiar language. Gulliver didn't understand much of it—in fact he could barely hear it, because the man's voice was so high and squeaky—but he did work out that they were going to take him prisoner and carry him back to their capital city. He decided it was best to do as they said. Meanwhile he made some signs to show that he would like some food. The little men had come prepared and started walking along his chest towards his mouth carrying meat, bread and wine. They had brought the biggest portions they could find—whole roast pigs and lambs, loaves of bread as big as their own heads and massive buckets of wine—but to Gulliver it was like eating crumbs and drinking out of a thimble.

After that they spent many hours building a wooden cart big enough to carry him away. They tied him to this cart and more than 1,000 of the strongest horses in the land pulled it towards the capital city. It took more than five hours, even though the city was only one kilometre away. At the edge of the city was a huge abandoned temple, and they decided that this would be a good place for Gulliver to sleep. They untied his cords and fastened his leg to the ground with a strong chain. Then he crawled into the temple, which was just big enough

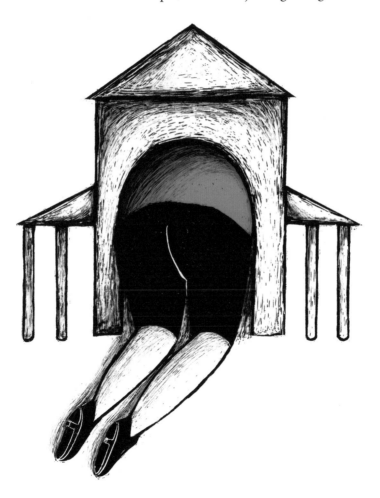

for him to squeeze through the door and lie full-length inside.

Stories about the arrival of this amazing giant soon spread throughout the city, and the next morning a huge crowd gathered to look at Gulliver when he crawled out of the temple. Most of them just stared at him, but five or six of the cruellest men started firing arrows into his face for fun. The police grabbed these men and asked Gulliver himself what he thought they should do with them. By way of reply, he picked up the men and stuffed all but one of them into his pocket. He brought the other one right up to his mouth, and opened his mouth wide as if he were going to eat him alive. But he was only pretending. Soon he put them all gently back down on the ground and the terrified men ran away.

The people all noticed how kind and merciful Gulliver had been, and everyone was talking about it afterwards. In fact, he had now made such a good impression on the people of this country that their Emperor decided to come and visit him.

Two

The country where Gulliver had found himself was called Lilliput. When the Emperor of Lilliput came to speak to him later that day, Gulliver found that he was a very impressive person, almost one centimetre taller than the other Lilliputians. He was about twenty-eight years old, and permitted Gulliver to hold him in the palm of his hand so that they could speak more easily.

Gulliver had already begun to learn some words in the Lilliputian language, and was able to understand that the Emperor was now offering to set him free and take off his chain. Gulliver was very happy about this.

The first thing he decided to do when he was set free was to take a walk around the capital city, and in particular to see the Emperor's palace. Walking along the main streets was like taking a tour round a miniature village. Even the tallest buildings only came up to his shoulders, and most of the streets were far too narrow for him to enter.

To get into the grounds of the Emperor's palace he had to step over a wall, and then to tread very carefully so that he didn't squash any of the hedges or the smaller buildings. When he stooped down and peered through the little windows, it was like looking into the most beautiful, expensive doll's house he had ever seen. He could see the Empress and the princes inside, and was very flattered when the Empress leant out of the window and offered him her tiny hand to kiss.

From now on, the Emperor was very friendly to Gulliver. He introduced him to many of the most important people at his court, and they spent a lot of time over the next few weeks sitting in the Imperial Gardens explaining all the laws and customs of Lilliput. Gulliver was always curious about this sort of thing and wanted to learn as much as possible. Some of the customs he thought were very odd. For instance, when the Lilliputians died they were buried in the ground, not lying down (as we Europeans are) but head first. This was because they believed that the world was flat, and in 1,000 years' time it would turn upside down, and all the dead people would come back to life again. So they wanted them to be standing the right way up when it happened.

Gulliver learnt that there was another island nearby, called Blefuscu, which was also inhabited by little people. He was surprised to hear that the two islands were at war with each other.

"What could you be fighting about?" he asked.

The Lilliputians told him that the two islands were at war over a very serious question. In Lilliput the people believed that, when you were eating a boiled egg, you should start by eating the little end. In Blefuscu they thought that you should eat the big end first. They had been fighting over this matter for three years now, and more than 60,000 people had died in the war.

"But that's ridiculous!" Gulliver said. Then the Emperor asked him whether his own country had ever gone to war over something so small. Gulliver thought about this, and had to admit that it often had.

He now thought of a way of pleasing the Emperor, who had shown him so much kindness. He offered to swim or even walk across to Blefuscu and capture their entire fleet, so that they wouldn't be able to threaten the Lilliputians any more.

The Emperor was delighted with this suggestion, and the next morning Gulliver set

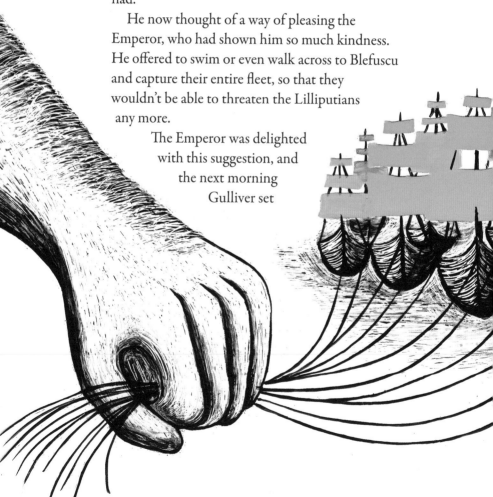

off on his mission. He waded through the water until his feet no longer touched the seabed, and then he swam the remaining distance to Blefuscu. As soon as he reached the harbour he saw at least forty warships there. The men on board were terrified to see this giant coming towards them, and they immediately jumped into the water and swam ashore. Meanwhile Gulliver reached into his bag and brought out the tools he had prepared already: lots of strong threads, each with a massive hook on the end. He placed a hook upon the prow of every ship, gathered the threads together and tried to pull the ships away with him. But the ships wouldn't move, because they had been securely anchored, so Gulliver had to take out his knife and cut every anchor rope. While he was doing this, the men standing on the harbour fired arrows continuously at his face. Gulliver wasn't much bothered by the stinging, although he did decide to put his glasses on in order to protect his eyes. Very soon he had finished his work and was able to pull the entire Blefuscu fleet away from the harbour and tow it in triumph all the way back to Lilliput.

Gulliver expected the Emperor to be very pleased—as indeed he was, at first. He conferred a very high honour on him, making him a knight or *Nardac* of the Lilliputian Empire. But when he asked Gulliver to return to Blefuscu and destroy all their remaining ships, and to kill or capture as many of the people as possible, Gulliver refused. He said it was wrong to invade a country of free people and kill them or turn them into slaves.

The Emperor was very annoyed when Gulliver disagreed with him about this. He was not used to being disobeyed. He said nothing about it at first, but his anger began to grow inside him. And this meant that from now on Gulliver's life in Lilliput was going to be very dangerous indeed.

Three

Gulliver had done a great service to the people of Lilliput by capturing the ships of their enemies. But afterwards he made a big mistake by criticizing the Emperor, and they began to mistrust each other.

Gulliver was starting to think that the Lilliputians were a crueller people than he had realized at first. And the Emperor was furious with him for making him feel like a harsh and tyrannical ruler. He began to think that the giant Gulliver was nothing but an expensive nuisance.

And in fact the Emperor had a point. Gulliver was very expensive to keep. He needed 300 cooks to prepare his food, and when he was eating he had twenty little waiters running about on his table, helping each other to carry the various dishes back and forth. Compared to a Lilliputian, he ate an enormous amount of food. He could easily eat several whole cows at one sitting—bones and all—and could fit dozens of miniature chickens onto his fork at once. He could guzzle down a whole barrel of Lilliputian wine and it would only feel as though he'd drunk a small glass.

One evening, as it happened, Gulliver had drunk two or three of these wine barrels and was just about to go to the toilet when he heard shouts in the street.

"Fire! Fire!" the people were calling. "The Emperor's palace is on fire!"

Gulliver strode over to the palace at once. Flames were tearing through the Imperial apartments and the firemen were facing a hopeless task, trying to put out the blaze with their tiny buckets of water.

Gulliver quickly realized that he could help. He was dying to go to the toilet anyway, so the simplest thing to do was to put out the fire that way. Maybe a few people would get splashed, and there would be a bit of a bad smell afterwards, but that was a price worth paying, wasn't it? Surely the important thing was to save the palace.

Because he'd had so much to drink, Gulliver
was able to go to the toilet non-stop for about two
minutes, and because he was careful to aim at the
parts of the palace where the fire was strongest, he
was able to put it out completely. What a relief! The
Emperor's beautiful building was saved!

Once again, he expected to be thanked for
helping the Emperor and his family. But in fact they
weren't pleased at all. From that day onwards the
Empress refused to go anywhere near the parts of
the palace which Gulliver had "contaminated" (as

she put it). And she wasn't the only one to make trouble. A number of the Emperor's advisers, who had been jealous of Gulliver for some time, used this incident as an excuse to begin plotting against him. They started whispering in the Emperor's ear that Gulliver might turn into an enemy of Lilliput, and that it was dangerous to keep him in the country any longer.

One night, after everyone was asleep, one important member of the Emperor's court, who was still loyal to Gulliver and remained his good friend, came into his room and told him that he would have to leave the country as quickly as possible. He revealed that the Emperor and his advisers had decided to make Gulliver harmless by blinding him.

Gulliver was horrified. At once he packed up his few possessions, and the next morning, at dawn, he escaped across the sea to the neighbouring island of Blefuscu, where only a few weeks earlier he had come to capture the fleet.

Although Gulliver had been their enemy in the recent war, the people of Blefuscu knew that he was a good man, because they had heard the story of how he had persuaded the Emperor of Lilliput not to kill or enslave them. Therefore they made him welcome, and offered him somewhere to stay for as long as he wanted. But Gulliver had learnt a hard lesson in Lilliput: he had learnt that it was a mistake to trust anyone but his best friends. He decided that he wanted to leave this part of the world altogether. He longed to return to a country where all the people were of his own size.

Luckily, after living for a few weeks in Blefuscu, he spotted a human-sized boat floating off the coast. It must have been washed up there after a shipwreck, he decided. Gulliver fitted it out for a short voyage and took with him enough food for a few weeks: that is, the bodies of 100 oxen and 300 sheep, hundreds of barrels of water and much more besides. He also took six live cows and sheep with him.

Gulliver set sail from Blefuscu on a warm day, in blazing sunshine, and this time he was lucky, because after only three days he spotted a full-size merchant ship on the horizon, and when the ship came closer he was invited to climb aboard. When he sat down to dinner with the Captain and his crew that evening, he could not get used to how big they all seemed. When he told them of his adventures in Lilliput they all looked at each other and laughed, assuming that drifting on the open seas in the sunshine for many weeks must have made Gulliver go completely mad. It was only when he took the six miniature cows and sheep out of his pocket and set them running around the table that everyone fell silent, their eyes wide with astonishment. After that they believed him.

Four

After his voyage to the tiny country of Lilliput, Gulliver was only at home with his wife and children for two months before he grew restless and decided to go travelling again. He got a job as a doctor on a ship that was bound for the East Indies, and set sail in the spring of 1702.

This time, the ship had travelled no further than the southern coast of Africa and the Cape of Good Hope when a terrible storm blew up. They were blown hundreds of kilometres in so many different directions that the sailors had no idea where they were any more. Finally the storm died down and they were able to weigh anchor off the coast of a large island. Some of the crew—including Gulliver—went ashore to look for food and water. While Gulliver was exploring by himself, he heard the other crew members shouting for help. He ran back to the beach and saw them rowing frantically back to the ship, pursued by a giant man. Compared to the sailors, this giant seemed just as big as Gulliver himself used to appear to the people of Lilliput.

The sailors got back onto their ship and managed to sail off before the giant could catch them. But that was no use to Gulliver. They had forgotten all about him, and now he was stranded and alone.

Frightened, he began to walk inland. He could tell that there was something strange about this island. Everything seemed enormous. The road he was walking along seemed ten times as wide as any road he'd seen before, and the grass on either side was so tall that it seemed to come up to his waist.

Before long he encountered two more of the giants

coming towards him
along the road. They were
wearing farm labourers'
clothes, and as soon as they
saw Gulliver they started to
chase him. He tried to escape
by running into the long grass
but one of them soon caught up
and snatched him with his big,
coarse hand. Gulliver was lifted at
least twenty metres into the air, and
he began shouting for mercy in a voice
as loud as he could make it, while putting his
hands together and begging to be treated kindly. At
this, the giant's face softened and he started to smile.
He put Gulliver carefully into his pocket and ran off
to show his discovery to his master, a farmer who
lived nearby.

The farmer lived in a nice old farmhouse with
his wife and daughter. When his servant came in
from the field to show Gulliver to him, he took
hold of the tiny man and placed him on the table,
staring at him for some time in wonder. Then his
wife and daughter came in. As soon as his wife

saw Gulliver she screamed at the top of her voice, thinking he must be some kind of mouse or big insect. The farmer calmed her down and then Gulliver himself ran over and apologized for scaring her. When they heard his squeaky voice talking in a foreign language, and saw him making a low bow, the farmer and his family could not stop themselves from bursting out laughing. The noise was so loud that Gulliver had to put his hands over his ears.

The farmer and his family sat down to lunch and allowed Gulliver to join them. They gave him a piece of meat which was about five times bigger than he was, and he began to cut it with his own little knife and fork, which he always carried with him. Again, everybody seemed to think this was hilarious. After a while Gulliver could hear some noises beneath the table, and then another noise close by: it was a loud rumbling noise. (To you and me, it would have sounded like the

revving of a hundred motorbikes.) It turned out to be the farmer's wife's cat, sitting on her mistress's lap and purring happily! When Gulliver leant over the edge of the table to look at the cat she spat at him and leapt up, lashing out at him with her terrible claws. He might easily have been killed if the farmer's daughter hadn't intervened, taking hold of the cat and shooing her out of the room, shutting the door safely in her face.

Gulliver thanked the farmer's daughter from the bottom of his heart. She was a pretty girl of about nine years old. Her name was Glumdalclitch and she would soon become his closest and most trusted friend in this new, frightening country.

Five

Gulliver stayed in the farmer's house for the next few days. He didn't want to go out or wander very far, because he was still getting used to the fact that everything around him was so large. In Lilliput he had felt like a god, towering over the puny citizens and holding them in the palm of his hand. Here in this new country (which was called Brobdingnag) he felt weak, insignificant and powerless.

He took comfort in the fact that Glumdalclitch was very kind to him. She persuaded her mother to let Gulliver sleep in the cradle she herself had used when she was a baby, and covered him with the finest, softest handkerchief she could find in the house—even though, for Gulliver, it felt as rough, big and heavy as sleeping underneath one of the sails from his ship.

When he woke up from his sleep one morning he learnt that the farmer was taking him on a trip. Gulliver was put in a wooden box (which Glumdalclitch took care to line with the quilt from her doll's bed) and then taken to the nearest market town in a pony-and-trap. Luckily his little friend came with him. Gulliver was terribly shaken about by the jogging of the pony and the bumps in the road: it was worse than the worst storm he had ever encountered at sea.

When they reached the town, he didn't much like what he found. It seemed the farmer had decided to make some money out of Gulliver by making him perform tricks on the table of an inn, charging the townspeople for the pleasure of seeing him. Thirty people came to watch each time, and Gulliver put on no fewer than twelve performances during that day: walking up and down the table, drawing his sword, dancing and speaking a few phrases in the Brobdingnagian language. The people laughed and applauded, until the noise was deafening.

"You could make even more
money out of him, I reckon," one of the farmer's
friends said to him. "Take him to the King's palace.
They would pay a fortune to have a creature like
that to amuse them at court."

The farmer wasted no time in acting upon this
suggestion. He drove to the palace the next day and
was quickly granted an audience, because the fame
of this peculiar little creature had already spread
to the King's court. He emerged from the royal
chamber looking very satisfied, with a big bag full
of gold coins. Meanwhile Gulliver was told that he
would be living in the royal palace from now on. He
asked if Glumdalclitch could stay there with him,
and luckily this request was granted.

Glumdalclitch was given her own set of rooms
in the royal palace, and the King's cabinet-maker

built Gulliver a lovely padded wooden box to live in, which was filled with miniature furniture. They were both very comfortable and happy. The Queen became devoted to him and would always insist that he sat beside her at the table whenever she took her meals.

Gulliver assumed that the King would also want to be entertained every day by watching him dance and perform tricks. But in fact, after their first meeting, the King did not ask to see Gulliver for some time. Instead he sent someone to teach him the language of Brobdingnag, and when Gulliver was finally able to speak it perfectly he was summoned back to the King to talk to him.

This King, you see, was a wise and intelligent ruler who was always very interested in the laws and customs of other countries, and he was extremely curious to hear Gulliver tell

him about this faraway land full of tiny people like himself. And Gulliver was delighted to be asked. He was a patriotic man, proud of his own country, and he couldn't wait to tell the King what wonderful places England and Europe were.

He began by describing the luxury in which the wealthiest people lived, the superb houses that they owned and the magnificent food which they were able to eat, imported from all over the world. The King was very impressed and asked if everybody lived like this. Gulliver said no—it was only a lucky few. Many people lived in poverty and hunger instead. But he said that even these people were able to buy luxury goods sometimes, by borrowing lots of money.

"So most people in your country live in debt?" the King asked, and Gulliver nodded.

But he said that by far the biggest expense was war, and one of the most glorious thing about the people of his country—in his opinion—was their willingness to spend vast amounts of money every year on armies and powerful weapons so that they could go to other faraway countries and get involved in wars that had nothing to do with them.

After giving this glowing account of affairs in his home country, Gulliver sat back and waited to hear what the King had to say. He was sure that he would be full of admiration.

But instead he looked very depressed for a few minutes, and then answered: "Gulliver, I like you very much. You are a good and civilized man. But as for the rest of your fellow countrymen, from what you have told me I can only conclude that they are the most pernicious race of little odious vermin ever suffered to crawl upon the surface of the earth."

There was a long silence while Gulliver stared back in astonishment. He could only ask himself: "Why on earth would the King think that?"

Six

Gulliver liked living in Brobdingnag, and he stayed there for more than three years. In all that time, he and Glumdalclitch were treated very kindly by almost everyone at court. The only person who did not like them was the Queen's dwarf. This cruel little man had always been treated like a celebrity because he was the smallest person in the country—until Gulliver came along. Now he was extremely jealous, and he did everything he could to make Gulliver's life difficult.

One day, for example, when Gulliver and Glumdalclitch were outside in the Royal Gardens, the dwarf waited until Gulliver was standing underneath an apple tree. Then he went over to the tree and started shaking the branches so that the apples came tumbling down onto Gulliver's back and head—each

one bigger and heavier than a
sack of potatoes. Poor Gulliver
might even have been killed if
he had not managed to dodge
most of the falling apples.
Another time the dwarf took
a handful of flies into
his hand and hurled
them into Gulliver's
face. These flies were as big
as blackbirds! Gulliver had
never seen anything so
disgusting, and he had
to fight them off with
his sword.

In fact he was often rather disgusted by the
things he saw. He came to realize that, when he
found something beautiful in his own country, it
was only because he was seeing it from the right
distance. Here in Brobdingnag he might be visited
by a lady who had the reputation of being the most
beautiful in town, and was amazed to see how
coarse and uneven her skin was, covered with thick
hairs and enormous pimples that were barely visible

to the other giants. And he had never seen anything so horrible as when he went on a tour of the capital city and he was taken close-up to see the beggars in the streets, with their terrible cancers and open wounds.

Another disadvantage of being so small was that he was in constant danger from the animals of Brobdingnag. The wasps, for instance, were all as big as birds and he could clearly see their long, sharp stings, which looked to him like daggers. Once, too, he was picked up by the royal gardener's pet spaniel and carried around the garden for about five minutes in its mouth. (Luckily it was a well-trained animal so it didn't bite Gulliver hard enough to kill him.) But the worst and saddest adventure of all happened one day when he and Glumdalclitch went to the seaside together.

They had just eaten a picnic lunch, and Gulliver was sleeping in his padded box while Glumdalclitch wandered off along the sandy beach to look for shells. Then, suddenly, Gulliver woke up with the most peculiar feeling. It was as if he weighed nothing at all, and meanwhile his box appeared to be swinging from side to side in the most alarming

manner. He ran to the window and looked out. He was horrified at what he saw: he was flying through the air, about 200 feet above the rough, stormy ocean! Then he looked up through the window and realized what had happened: a huge golden eagle had caught hold of his box on the beach, lifted the handle in its beak and was flying away with it. The bird was probably planning to dash it against some rocks and then eat the little creature who was hiding inside.

But Gulliver's box was heavy—too heavy for this eagle, it seemed. Without any warning, the eagle opened its beak with a loud cry and let the box plummet down towards the waves. It sank almost to the bottom and then floated back up to the surface. Gulliver was still alive, but he was now adrift on the open seas, many miles from the shore. He wept to think that he would never see his beloved Glumdalclitch again.

The next day, when Gulliver was almost dead from starvation and thirst, he spied a ship on the horizon. The ship came closer and when they saw what appeared to be a large floating wooden room bobbing up and down on the waves, the sailors on board were quite amazed. They were even more amazed when Gulliver called out to them: "Please, one of you, pick up this box by the handle, and carry me on board!" How were they supposed to pick up something as big as that? They thought he was mad. But Gulliver had simply forgotten what it was like to be back among normal-sized people again.

And indeed, after the kind sailors on this ship had finally taken him back to England, it was many months before he could get used to the size of the people and the buildings in London. He kept thinking that he was in Lilliput again—a giant, walking like a colossus among crowds of tiny men and women.

Seven

After his adventures in Brobdingnag—
adventures which had almost cost
him his life—Gulliver resolved that
he would never go to sea again. He
decided to stay at home with his wife
and children.

One day, however, a merchant came to him with
an offer that he couldn't refuse. He proposed that
Gulliver should take to the ocean again, but not as a
doctor this time—as the captain of his own ship. He
offered a lot of money, and after much hesitation
Gulliver agreed. He only hoped that he would have
better luck than on his last two voyages.

But once again, fortune was not on Gulliver's
side. After he had been travelling for many months
and had almost sailed as far as Japan, his ship was
attacked by pirates. They took Gulliver prisoner
and then set him adrift in a small open boat with
only enough food and water for three days. They
assumed that he would die; but of course, they had
underestimated Gulliver and his will to survive.

Gulliver managed to steer his little boat towards a small rocky island, and he stayed there for several days, living off the birds' eggs which he found in the nests among the rocks. Then, one morning, a huge shadow passed over the sun. Gulliver looked up towards the sky and saw one of the most surprising things he had yet encountered on his travels. It was an island—a whole island, about five kilometres across—and it was flying over him. Flying through the sky!

There were balconies on the side of the island, with staircases running between them. A lot of people were gathered on the balconies because they had spotted Gulliver and wanted to rescue him. Some of the people ran off to get a very long rope ladder which they carefully let down, so that Gulliver could climb up it to join them.

When he had safely climbed up onto one of the balconies, the people all crowded round Gulliver and seemed very excited to see him. But then, after a few minutes, most of them lost interest and wandered off.

He thought that this was strange. They all had very wise and clever faces, but they were also very

clumsy: they kept tripping over
stones in the road, and walking into
lamp-posts, as if they were finding it
hard to concentrate on where they
were going. Finally Gulliver managed
to persuade someone to conduct him to the King.

He was taken to a very grand chamber in the
royal palace, where he found the King surrounded

by courtiers and attendants, all of whom were wearing cloaks embroidered with mathematical symbols and astronomical signs. The King showed no sign that he had noticed Gulliver's arrival, as he seemed to be busy with a very long and complicated mathematical calculation. At last he solved it, after about an hour and after using up dozens of sheets of paper. It was only then that he looked up and realized that Gulliver had been brought to see him.

One of the attendants began to explain how they had found Gulliver and rescued him, but the King stopped concentrating after a minute or two and did not listen to most of the speech. He gave brief instructions that Gulliver should be made welcome, and given a room and some food, but after that he went back to his calculations.

Over the next few days Gulliver came to learn that this was normal behaviour among the inhabitants of the flying island (which was called Laputa). They were so busy thinking about maths, music and astronomy that they completely forgot about all the practical things that had to be done every day. They even had to keep servants with them all the time, called flappers. These servants always

carried a balloon fixed upon the end of a stick, and
their job was to hit their masters in the face with
these balloons every time they lost concentration
because they were too busy having brilliant
thoughts.

Gulliver thought that the Laputans must be very
clever indeed, if their heads were so full of fine ideas
that they kept forgetting where they were or what
they were supposed to be doing. After a few days,
therefore, he decided to find out more about their
science and learning, by accepting an invitation to
visit the University of Laputa.

Eight

The university was a very grand building
in the middle of the flying island.
Gulliver was curious to know what the
people were studying there. He had
already noticed that the Laputans were
obsessed with mathematics: for instance,
at dinner time their food was always
cut into triangles, circles and cuboids,
and when they needed to have some
clothes made they went to a geometry
professor rather than a tailor (which
might possibly explain why none of their
clothes ever seemed to fit).

But what else were they interested in, he wondered.
When he began his tour, the first person he met
was a crazy-looking old man locked in a tiny room
surrounded by scientific equipment. He was told that
this man was working on an experiment to extract

sunlight out of cucumbers. There were hundreds of
sliced and mashed-up old cucumbers on the ground
all around him. So far he had been working on
the experiment for forty years, without any sign of
success at all. But he was sure that he would make a
breakthrough in the next year or two.

Another man was engaged upon a scheme which
would make it possible for people from different
countries to understand each other completely,
without the need for a translator: he was planning

to abolish words altogether. This man's reasoning was that, since all *words* are just substitutes for *things*, it would be easier for people simply to carry with them all the things they needed to express themselves. So far, it was true, the main problem had been that anyone who wanted to have an interesting, wide-ranging conversation with another person needed to carry such a big sack of objects with them that it was enough to break their back. But this, he was convinced, was just a minor difficulty, which he hoped to solve very soon.

Another professor was working on a scheme to make teaching much easier. Instead of giving his students lessons, he proposed to write down his ideas on small pieces of paper and get his students to eat them—after doing without food for three days, in order to aid digestion. Unfortunately the only students who had tried this method so far had ended up being violently sick. But, like his colleagues, this professor was not discouraged and was determined to carry on with his experiment until it worked.

After spending a few hours at the university Gulliver was beginning to think that all the

Laputans were quite mad, and he was on the point of asking whether they would lend him another rope ladder so that he could leave the island. But then he heard about something else that he was curious to see. Apparently, there was a special group of Laputans who were born with a red mark upon their foreheads, which meant that they were marked out for a unique privilege: they were immortal, and would never have to die. These people were known as the Struldbrugs, and Gulliver couldn't wait to meet them and talk to them. He was convinced that they must be the happiest people in the world, knowing that they would never die. And not just the happiest, but the wisest, for they would have witnessed hundreds of years of human history, and must have learnt a great deal from all the mistakes that mankind had made in the past. Probably, Gulliver thought, they would all occupy very important positions in the government, so that the King and his ministers could all benefit from their wisdom.

Alas, he found that the truth was quite the opposite. It turned out that the Struldbrugs were the saddest and loneliest people he had ever met.

Most of them were over 200 years old, but they had all lost their memories when they were about eighty, so they could not tell him anything interesting; some of them could not even remember how to speak. They had also lost their sense of taste and smell so they could not get any pleasure from eating or drinking. The Struldbrugs hated all young people, because they envied their good health and vitality. And they also hated each other, because each one reminded the other of his miserable condition. None of the other islanders liked to spend time with them, of course—partly because they were so bad-tempered and gloomy all the time, but mainly because they were so ghastly to look at, with their shrivelled, wrinkly skin hanging loosely from their bones, and their terrible sunken eyes staring out at the world with a mixture of horror and dreadful boredom.

Gulliver could not wait to get away from the Struldbrugs. They made him realize something that had never occurred to him before. He had always been afraid of dying, and had always regarded death as a wretched misfortune. But now he realized that death could also be a release, and the gateway to a kind of freedom. Nothing could be worse than being condemned to stay on this earth for ever, alone, missing your loved ones and thinking about them for long years after they had departed.

These creatures appalled him so much that he told the Laputans he wanted to leave the flying island as soon as possible. He asked if they could let down a rope ladder for him as soon as the island was flying over some country where lots of people lived, so that he could obtain passage on a ship that was returning back to England. They told him that, by a stroke of good luck, the island was presently flying over Japan.

And so, that very afternoon, Gulliver was escorted down to one of the balconies, a rope ladder was thrown over the side for him, and he climbed down as swiftly as he could, leaving this island and its peculiar inhabitants behind for ever.

Nine

At the bottom of the ladder Gulliver jumped down onto a long, white, sandy beach. The ladder was pulled up after him, and he waved goodbye to the assembled Laputans, although they took little notice. Probably they were already too busy thinking about some new mathematical problem.

As soon as he had this thought, a nasty suspicion crossed Gulliver's mind. Was this country really Japan? The Laputans were useless at most practical things, and most likely they were not very good at navigation. This new land seemed to be quite deserted. Gulliver had seen pictures of Japan in books, and it didn't look anything like this at all.

Gulliver was quite right. In fact he was thousands of miles from Japan. By the end of that day he would discover that he was in a country where no human being had ever set foot before.

In the meantime, he left the beach and began to

walk inland. He walked for several miles through
a barren landscape without seeing a single living
creature. And then, suddenly, he saw a herd of
animals gathered in a field by the side of the road.
They were standing on two legs and looked almost
human, except that they were wearing no clothes,
and they had long claws and hair all over their
bodies. They were fighting over a scrap of meat,
howling and jabbering at each other in horrible

harsh voices and
tearing at each
other with their
claws. Gulliver
shivered and
hurried on. He had
never seen creatures
which filled him with
such fear and horror
before.

Shortly afterwards,
he met two horses coming down the road towards
him. The horses stopped and stared at Gulliver with
wise, gentle faces. He tried to stroke one of them,
but the horse backed away. Then the two horses
started neighing to each other. Their neighs were so
complicated and expressive that Gulliver began to
suspect the two horses were actually talking to each
other in some strange language of their own.

After walking around Gulliver for a few minutes
and examining him carefully, the horses made a gesture
with their heads to say that he should come with them.
He followed them for about two miles, until they
came to a large building in the middle of a field.

The building had a straw roof and inside it was rather like a stable, but cleaner and tidier. This seemed to be where one of the horses lived with his family. They welcomed Gulliver inside and then had a long conversation, in which he kept hearing the word "Yahoo". Then they took him outside into the backyard, where he saw three more of those horrible creatures chained up to a tree, once again fighting over food.

"Yahoo," the horses kept saying, pointing with their hooves from Gulliver to these hateful animals.

Suddenly he realized their meaning.

"*NO!* I'm not one of *them*!" he shouted in horror. "I'm a man. A human being!"

Well, the horses could certainly see that Gulliver was very different to these creatures in some respects, so they allowed him to sleep in their stable that night, and the next morning started giving him lessons in horse language. Gulliver had always been good at learning languages, so after a couple of weeks he was able to hold a good conversation with the horses. One of the first things he learnt was that they called themselves Houyhnhnms.

Gulliver quickly came to like his "Master" (as he called the horse who was allowing him to live in his house) very much indeed. Everything he did seemed to be reasonable, orderly and civilized. He kept a clean house, and never seemed to get angry or upset about anything. Gulliver spent as much time as he could with his Master, and never went near the revolting Yahoos or had anything to do with them.

Gulliver's Master was perplexed by his new guest. In shape he looked just like a Yahoo. But he also wore clothes, and could learn languages, and liked to cook his food, and didn't seem to be nearly as cruel or savage as the Yahoos were. So what kind of creature was he, exactly?

Gulliver did his best to explain things to him. He explained that in the country he came from, all of the people were shaped like Yahoos, and walked upright on their back legs. But they were very different in every other way: they were clever and civilized, they spoke to each other in lots of different languages, they wrote books and poems, had a genius for mathematics and science, were brilliant at inventing things, and they didn't fight with each other all the time.

As soon as he said this, however, Gulliver realized that it was not strictly true. Of course, human

beings did have fights with each other—terrible fights—but they weren't called "fights", they were called "wars". And since the Houyhnhnms didn't have a word for "war" in their language, Gulliver had to explain what it was. For one thing, his Master couldn't understand how someone like Gulliver—whose nails weren't nearly as long as the Yahoos' claws—could be capable of hurting anyone at all. So Gulliver had to tell him what guns were. And not just guns, but cannons, bombs and every kind of explosive device. It took a long time to explain, and when it was finished his Master looked truly upset.

"You mean that with all your cleverness, and all your wisdom, there are still men who use their time, and their brains, making things which are designed to kill people? And not just some people, but as many people as possible? Is there really such evil in your world?"

After this conversation, Gulliver's Master went away to a quiet part of the stable and thought for a long time about what he had learnt. Gulliver watched him, and for the first time in his life felt ashamed of himself and his fellow humans.

Epilogue

Despite his disappointment at learning what the human species was capable of, Gulliver's Master allowed him to stay in his home and they became good friends. The Houyhnhnms remained curious about this odd creature who seemed to be almost-but-not-really a Yahoo, and Gulliver for his part came to love his Master very much.

Whether that love was actually returned, it was difficult to say. One of the things that Gulliver noticed about the Houyhnhnms was that they never really seemed to feel much emotion. Everything they did, they did because it was sensible, not because they were moved to do it by their feelings. And so, for instance, although they cared for their foals well, a mother and father would treat their own children no differently than they would the children of another family, and never showed them any particular affection. In the same way, they showed no particular grief when the eldest horses died. They just accepted it. When two horses decided to become husband and wife, it was never because they loved each other, but because their appearances were well suited to each other, and they were likely to produce strong, handsome children.

Gulliver could not help feeling that, in these areas at least, the Houyhnhnm way of doing things was rather cold. Much as he admired these calm, reasonable horses, he wondered whether human beings, for all their faults, possibly enjoyed life more than they did.

On the whole, though, he was extremely glad to be in the country of the Houyhnhnms, where he lived for two very happy years. In that time, just as he came to like the horses more and more, so his hatred of the Yahoos grew stronger and stronger. And what made it worse was realizing that he resembled them in many respects. One day, for instance, his Master described to him something that the horses had always found puzzling about the Yahoos: that they loved to dig up shiny, brightly coloured stones from the earth, and would then put piles of them away carefully in secret hiding places, often spending hours looking at them and counting them and guarding them jealously. If another Yahoo tried to steal any of these stones away, the most terrible fight would ensue. What could it mean, the Master Houyhnhnm wanted to know? Gulliver could not give him a satisfactory explanation, but could only tell him that human beings had a similar love and obsession for these brightly coloured stones—which they called by the name money.

Because he spent so much time with Gulliver, the Master Horse could see that he was very different from the Yahoos in many ways; but the other Houyhnhnms disagreed, and they thought it was wrong that he should be keeping a Yahoo in his house with him. One day, therefore, after a long meeting of the Houyhnhnm parliament, it was decided that Gulliver would have to leave their country and make his way back to the land he had come from.

Gulliver was heartbroken. He could not bear the thought of leaving these wise and gentle creatures behind and spending the rest of his life among Yahoos. (For this was how even he had started to think of his fellow humans.) But his protests

were ignored. He had to build himself a canoe and then, taking with him enough provisions to last for several weeks, he set sail onto the open seas again.

Gulliver did not want to go back to England. If he was not allowed to live with the Houyhnhnms any more, he decided that he would rather live alone. So he steered his canoe towards a deserted island, and moored it in a creek while he went to look for more food and water.

When he got back to his boat he found that it was surrounded by men. They were Portuguese sailors from a large trading ship which had been passing by. They seized hold of Gulliver and asked him what he was doing there. He answered them as best he could, but they could hardly understand a word he was saying. To them, it sounded like the neighing of a horse! They burst out laughing and concluded that he must be mad.

They forced Gulliver to come back with them onto their ship and took him to see their captain. He was a kind and intelligent man, and he could see at once that Gulliver was very distressed. In fact Gulliver could scarcely bear to be in the presence of all these Yahoos. He hated the very sight and smell of them, and asked to be given his own cabin where he could rest undisturbed. And that was where he stayed for the rest of the voyage home.

Poor Gulliver! When he got back from the first of his travels, back from the miniature country of Lilliput, everything in England had seemed enormous. When he returned from Brobdingnag, the land of the giants, everything had seemed tiny. But it was far worse coming home from the country of the Houyhnhnms. Everywhere he looked he saw people: people who reminded him of those dirty, aggressive, savage Yahoos. Their very smell was horrible to him. Even his own family reminded him of Yahoos! For the first few years after he returned, Gulliver didn't even want to live in the same house as they. Instead he went to live in the stable at the bottom of his garden, and bought two horses to keep him company. They did not speak the horse language as well as Gulliver's Master back in the beloved Houyhnhnm country, but still, it was better than nothing.

It was a year before Gulliver could bear to sit down at the same table as his wife and children, and eat the same food as they. Every day he looked at them and asked himself the same question, over and over: "What kind of creatures are they, this woman, and this little boy and girl? What are they closest to? Are they closest to the Yahoos, or to the Houyhnhnms? Which ones are they?"

And sometimes there was an even more frightening question that he asked himself: "Which one am I?"

For Matilda and Madeline

WHERE IS THIS
STORY FROM?

Jonathan Swift was born more than 350 years ago. He died in 1745, when he was seventy-seven years old. As well as being a writer and a poet, he was also a priest—he held the title of Dean of St Patrick's, a beautiful cathedral in Dublin.

Dublin is in Ireland and Jonathan Swift, although he is often referred to as an English writer, was born in Ireland and lived there for most of his life. He believed that the English people treated the Irish people very badly, and he often used his writing to do whatever he could to help the Irish people and keep them from poverty and hunger.

Swift spent five years writing the story of *Gulliver's Travels*. It was finally published in 1726 and became an immediate best-seller. All the copies were sold within the first week.

Jonathan Swift once said that he wrote *Gulliver's Travels* "in order to vex the world, rather than divert it". What he meant was that, although he knew it was an entertaining story, that was not his main reason for writing it. He wrote it to make people think. He wanted them to think about the political issues of the time—such as warfare and poverty—but he also wanted them to think about something even larger and more important: human nature. By the end of the book, he wanted people to be asking themselves questions like "Are human beings good, or evil? Should we do things because they are sensible and reasonable, or for other reasons?"

Like many of the greatest stories and works of literature, *Gulliver's Travels* is not a book which sets out to provide answers; it aims only to ask interesting and important questions.

J. C.

JONATHAN COE was born 57 years ago in England, where he still lives. He has written many books, among them *What a Carve Up!*, *The Rotters' Club* and *Middle England*, but knows he will never write one as good as *Gulliver's Travels*.

SARA ODDI was born in Ascoli Pieno in 1984. Ever since she was little, she entertained herself by inventing and illustrating stories. She lives in a small village near her birthplace and, although a few years have passed since then, this remains her great passion, together with good Marchesian food.

SAVE THE STORY is a library of favourite stories from around the world, retold for today's children by some of the best contemporary writers. The stories they retell span cultures (from Ancient Greece to nineteenth-century Russia), time and genres (from comedy and romance to mythology and the realist novel), and they have inspired all manner of artists for many generations.

Save the Story is a mission in book form: saving great stories from oblivion by retelling them for a new, younger generation.

THE SCUOLA HOLDEN (Holden School) was born in Turin in 1994. At the School one studies "storytelling", namely the secret of telling stories in all possible languages: books, cinema, television, theatre, comic strips—with extravagant results.

This series is dedicated to Achille, Aglaia, Arturo, Clara, Kostas, Olivia, Pietro, Samuele, Sandra, Sebastiano and Sofia.

PUSHKIN CHILDREN'S BOOKS

We created Pushkin Children's Books to share tales from different languages and cultures with younger readers, to open the door to the wide, colourful worlds these stories offer.

From picture books and adventure stories to fairy tales and classics, and from fifty-year-old bestsellers to current huge successes abroad, the books on the Pushkin Children's list reflect the very best stories from around the world, for our most discerning readers of all: children.

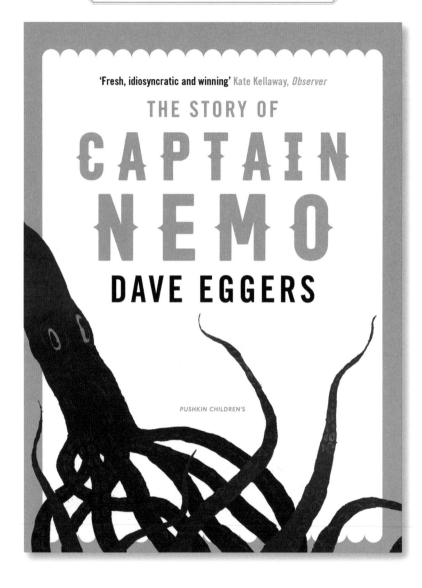

'Fresh, idiosyncratic and winning' Kate Kellaway, *Observer*

THE STORY OF

CAPTAIN

NEMO

DAVE EGGERS

PUSHKIN CHILDREN'S

The Story of

ANTIGONE

ALI SMITH

'Amazing'
Daily Telegraph

'Brilliantly told… beautiful'
Observer

PUSHKIN CHILDREN'S